Albert and Sarah Jane

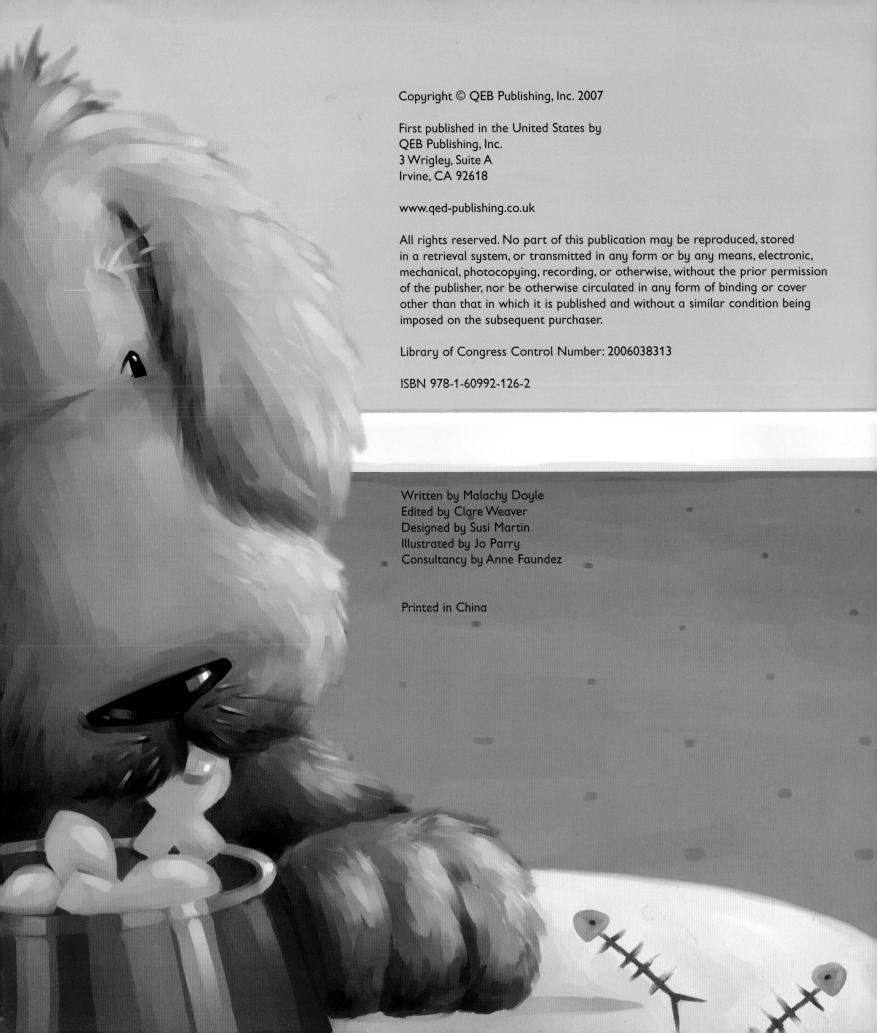

First published in the United States by
QEB Publishing, Inc.
3 Wrigley, Suite A
Irvine, CA 92618

www.qed-publishing.co.uk

Library of Congress Control Number: 2006038313

ISBN 978-1-60992-126-2

Written by Malachy Doyle
Edited by Clare Weaver
Designed by Susi Martin
Illustrated by Jo Parry
Consultancy by Anne Faundez

Printed in China

Albert and Sarah Jane

Malachy Doyle

Illustrated by Jo Parry

QEB Publishing

Albert and Sarah Jane were the very best of friends. Their favorite thing to do was curl up in a great big cat-dog cuddle by the fire.

But there was one thing Albert liked even better than that.

And that was eating his yummy, scrummy crunchies from his big blue bowl.

And there was one thing he liked even better than **that**.
And that was eating Sarah Jane's even
yummier, scrummier fishy nibbles.

He'd steal one or two from
her little red bowl when his
friend wasn't looking. They
always tasted so much
better than his own!

But one morning, while Sarah Jane was out and about, Albert got a little carried away with his nibbling.

When his friend came back in from the yard,
she was all ready for breakfast. But there wasn't
a speck of food left in her little red bowl.

When Sarah Jane looked to see if there was anything in Albert's big blue bowl...

she found there wasn't a speck of food there, either!

She went to ask Albert why there wasn't any
food to eat, but he was fast asleep in his basket.

That's odd, she thought, I'm sure he's fatter than usual.
And I'm sure he smells all fishy, too!

"You've been eating my food, you naughty dog!" hissed Sarah Jane, arching her back.

But Albert just snored and ignored her.

"Okay," said Sarah Jane.
"I've had enough of this!"

She turned around and
marched straight
out of the house.

Albert opened one
eye and saw Sarah Jane
leaving through the pet door.

She'll be back, he thought.
She always comes back.

But Sarah Jane didn't come back.
She went to live next door instead.

By that evening, Albert was
lonely. By the next morning,
he was howling at the pet door.

"Come home, Sarah Jane!"
he cried.

I miss you!

Albert spotted Sarah Jane
through the upstairs window.

He smiled at her, in a doggy
sort of way, but Sarah Jane
ignored him.

So Albert sneaked out of the house, went next door, sat himself down on the doorstep, and howled.

"Come home, Sarah Jane!" he cried.

I miss you!

"Stop howling, you naughty dog!"
hissed Sarah Jane, coming down
to see what all the fuss was about.

"But I'm sad and lonely," said Albert.
"I want a great big cat-dog cuddle by the fire."

"Well, the food's better over here and nobody steals it," said Sarah Jane.

"But it's lonely here, too, without a big, smelly lump of a dog to snuggle up to..."